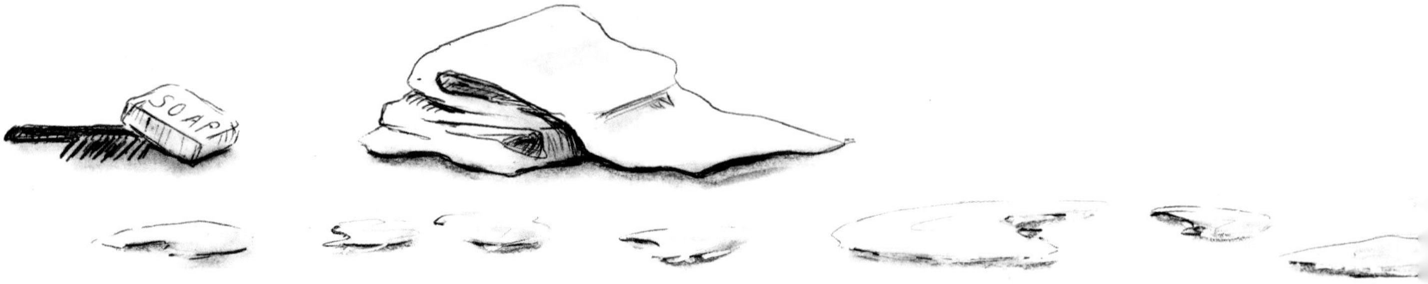
SOAP

Gulliver Snip

Julia Kay

HOLT AND COMPANY

NEW YORK

Henry Holt and Company, LLC
Publishers since 1866
175 Fifth Avenue
New York, New York 10010
www.HenryHoltKids.com

Library of Congress Cataloging-in-Publication Data
Kay, Julia.
Gulliver Snip / Julia Kay.—1st ed.
p.   cm.
Summary: A little boy has grand, swashbuckling adventures at bathtime
in his clipper ship—the bathtub.
ISBN-13: 978-0-8050-7992-0 / ISBN-10: 0-8050-7992-0
[1. Baths—Fiction. 2. Bathtubs—Fiction. 3. Pirates—Fiction. 4. Clipper
ships—Fiction. 5. Imagination—Fiction. 6. Stories in rhyme.] I. Title.
PZ8.3.K223Gul 2008   [E]—dc22   2007002828

First Edition—2008 / Designed by Amelia May Anderson
The artist used acrylic and pastel on paper to create the illustrations
for this book.
Printed in the United States of America on acid-free paper. ∞

10 9 8 7 6 5 4 3 2 1

For those who take adventures
instead of taking baths

Gulliver Snip had a clipper ship
that his mother called the bathtub.

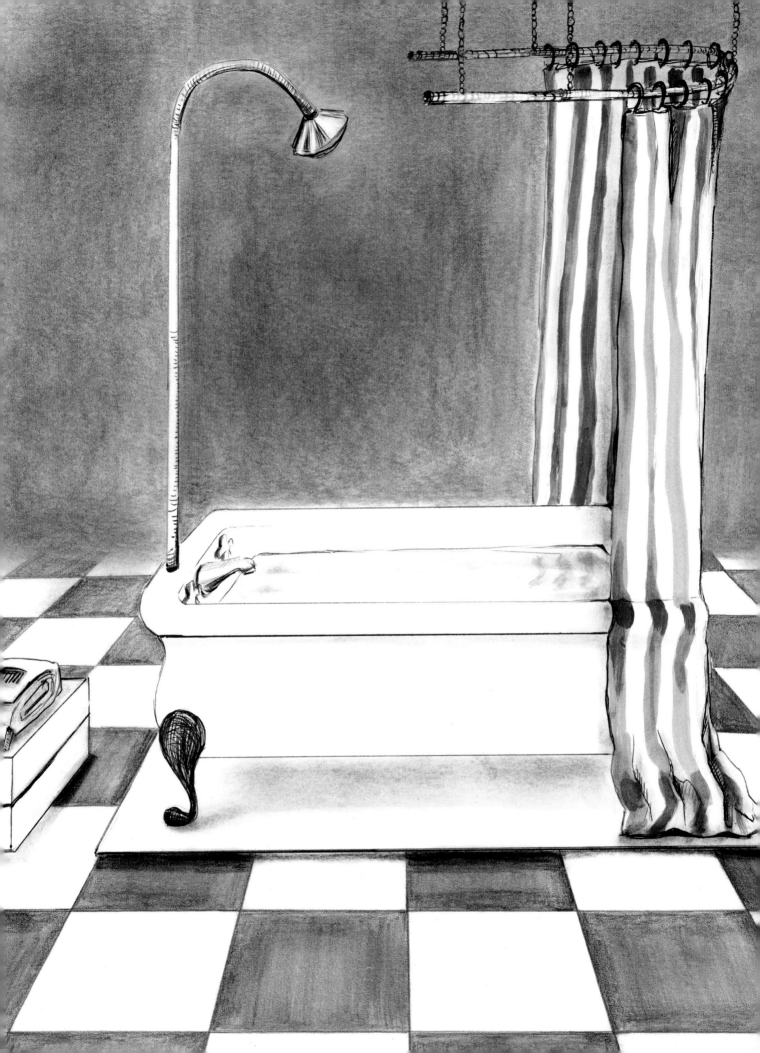

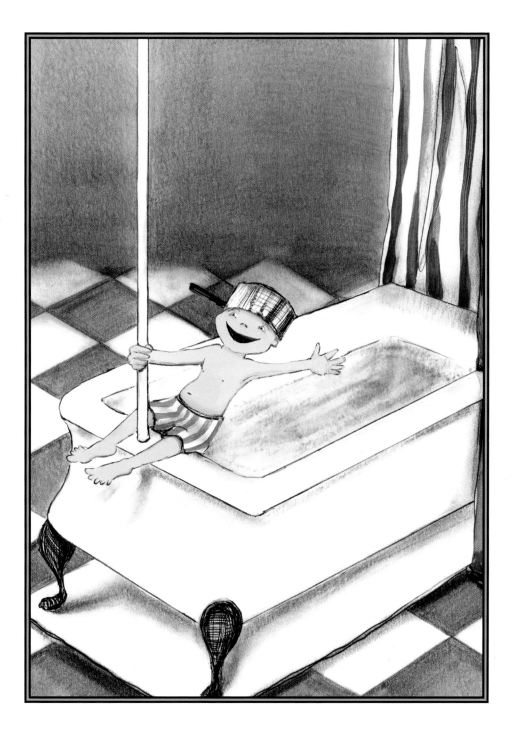

And every night Captain Gulliver Snip
took a trip in his wonderful clipper ship
that his mother called the bathtub.

The storms would rage,
the waves would swell.
"Man the ropes!" young Snip would yell
till the mighty mast and sail fell
on that dangerous trip in the clipper ship
that his mother called the bathtub.

Once, stronger winds began to whip
and water filled the clipper ship,
but Captain Snip began to bail
the water out with a garbage pail
in the raging, blowing, stormy gale
on the dangerous trip in the clipper ship
that his mother called the bathtub.

Soon Snip knew his ship was sunk,
so he leapt overboard in a packing trunk
and he surged up a wave with a whoop and a yell.
On the curl of its crest he rode that swell,
and looking back, Snip waved farewell
to the sinking ship, the clipper ship
that his mother called the bathtub.

Through an arch and down the hall
of a well-lit cave with a waterfall
Snip rode the wave—he braved it all
in his packing trunk
for his ship was sunk,
the wonderful ship, the clipper ship
that his mother called the bathtub.

At last "LAND HO!" Snip loudly cried,
when he saw the break of the surging tide
on the sand of a land that was wild and wide,
which he hit with a clunk
in his packing trunk
for his ship was sunk,
the wonderful ship, the clipper ship
that his mother called the bathtub.

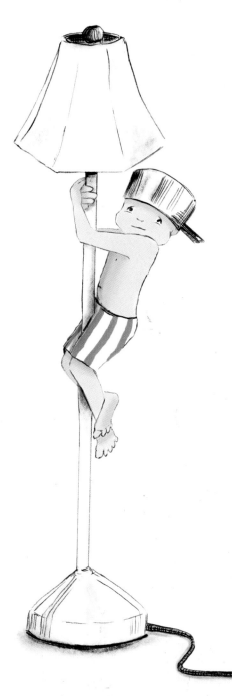

All washed up and worn from sea,
Snip dragged himself up a coconut tree
and saw from the top, to his great dismay,
a tiger heading fast his way!

Just then the tree began to sway,
and sway,
and sway, and—CRASH!—
Snip fell with the lamp to the rug,
where his mother scooped him up in a hug
and said to her boy, while she held him snug . . .

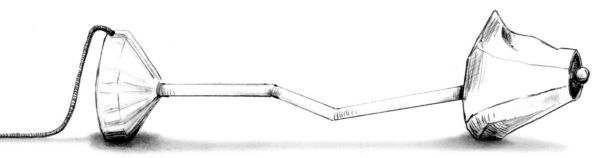

"The hall is wet, the stairs are damp,
and someone broke my favorite lamp.
That someone also drenched the den
and overflowed the tub again.
Gulliver Snip, did you make this mess?"
And Snip, feeling sorry, with a sigh, said, "Yes."

Though he squirmed, he could not escape
(for Captain Snip was in shabby shape).
Mother wrapped him in his captain's cape
and dried him off from his toes to his tip,
then sent him to bed with a smooch on the lip . . .

. . . where bravest Captain Gulliver Snip
dreamed all about tomorrow's trip
when the waves would swell and the winds would whip
and he'd brave the storm in his clipper ship . . .

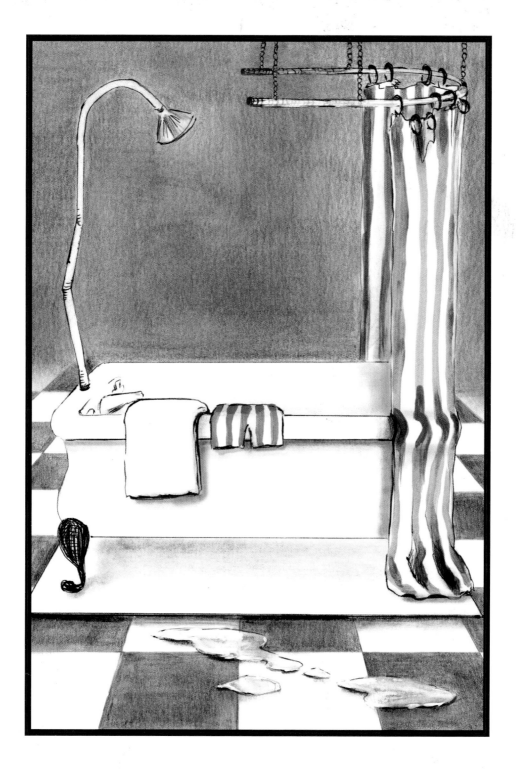

. . . the wonderful, marvelous clipper ship
that his mother called the bathtub.

THE CHILDREN'S BIBLE

Volume 10

A Golden Press / Funk & Wagnalls, Inc. Book
Published by Western Publishing Company, Inc.

Distributed by Funk & Wagnalls, Inc. New York

Library of Congress Catalog Card Number: 81-81439

ISBN 0-8343-0047-8 (Volume 10)
ISBN 0-8343-0037-0 (12 Volume Set)

CONTENTS

JESUS PREACHES ON FORGIVENESS 588
Jesus shames the scribes and the Pharisees into releasing
an accused woman when he says that whoever is without
sin should cast the first stone.

JESUS PREACHES IN PARABLES 592
A multitude gathers on the seashore to hear Jesus speak.

JESUS IN NAZARETH 596
The people of Nazareth drive Jesus, the son of a carpenter,
from the city because he claims to be the fulfillment of the
Scriptures.

THE BEHEADING OF JOHN THE BAPTIST 600
King Herod is tricked into killing John the Baptist to please
his wife and stepdaughter.

THE FEEDING OF THE MULTITUDE 602
From only two small fishes and five loaves of barley, Jesus
feeds a large crowd of his followers.

JESUS INSTRUCTS THE DISCIPLES 608
Jesus tells his disciples the parables of the good Samaritan
and the prodigal son to teach them forgiveness and to
strengthen their faith.

THE JOURNEY TO JERUSALEM 620
Jesus raises his friend Lazarus from the dead, telling his
disciples: "He that believes in me, though he is dead, shall
live."

ILLUSTRATED GLOSSARY 627
Notes, definitions, illustrations, and maps.

INTRODUCTION

The message Jesus wanted to bring to men and women was not easy to understand, so Jesus used stories, called parables, as a way of explaining himself to the people. In the parables he used examples and places that the people could recognize. Jesus could do this because he had grown up in a poor family in Nazareth and was familiar with everyday life in Palestine. When Jesus spoke of a tiny mustard seed that would grow into a great tree, all the farmers listening to Jesus knew how small a mustard seed was, and so they could begin to understand what Jesus was trying to say.

Jesus knew that the people could not easily understand his parables. He wanted the people to go home and think about the stories and to try to figure out what he was saying. Usually it took a lot of hard work to understand what a parable meant, but doing this work was part of being a follower of Jesus.

Some of the people listening to Jesus never understood the parables. This was not because Jesus wanted to hide his teaching from them; he was willing to explain his stories to his disciples and to all men and women who really wanted to understand him. The people who did not understand the parables did not want to understand them. They were unwilling to try, so they did not listen to Jesus.

Jesus taught his followers in other ways besides preaching in parables. He performed miracles to show them how great God was. He wanted to tell the people that God was more powerful than sickness or death, so Jesus healed the sick, gave blind people sight, and brought the dead back to life. Because the Jews believed that sickness came from a very strong evil force, Jesus' power of healing showed the people that there was no greater power than God's.

Through his compassion for them, Jesus showed the sick and the blind that God loved them and would protect them. And for the Christians who retold these stories of Jesus' healing, the miracles showed that Jesus was God's son and shared God's power. Jesus revealed who he was by working these miracles.

Jesus, however, did not work miracles in order to prove that he was the Son of God. In fact, he did not like it when people believed in him only because they had seen one of his miracles — he wanted them to have faith in him without needing the miracles as proof. Jesus performed the miracles because he

loved all men and women and because he wanted them to know that something new and great was happening in their time. Christians believe that through Jesus, God once again showed his presence on Earth, just as he had during the time of Moses and the exodus. The miracles were a sign that God was among his people, just as April flowers are a sign that spring has come.

Christians say that Jesus came to bring the Kingdom of God to Earth. This Kingdom is not an actual place and it is not a special kind of government. It is a new way for men and women to love and respect each other. The Kingdom of God is a way of loving and living with a changed heart.

Christians believe that the doors of the Kingdom were first opened when Jesus began preaching among the people. They say that Jesus' death and resurrection made the Kingdom very strong and great. Christians also believe that men and women cannot live completely in the Kingdom until Jesus returns to the Earth, but they can make a good start now by living as Jesus told them to live.

Before they could enter the Kingdom, Jesus said that his disciples had to repent. He wanted them to give up everything that distracted them from turning their full attention to God. This is why Jesus told the rich man to give up his riches: he knew that as long as the rich man loved and depended upon his money, he would never fully love and depend upon God. Jesus wanted men and women to be free to love God, so he invited them to give up everything that kept them from God and from each other.

Jesus gave his followers many clues about how to live in the Kingdom of God. He told them that they had to be as obedient as little children; that they had to be merciful to one another; and that they should forgive one another. Their love for each other had to be like the love of the Samaritan man for the wounded traveler. Even though the Samaritan did not know the injured man, he did not hesitate to help him.

It was not easy being a disciple of Jesus, because he demanded that his followers put their trust completely in God. When Jesus called his disciples to follow him, he wanted them to drop what they were doing and obey him. He wanted them to change their whole lives. And he wanted them to do this right away, because the Kingdom of God was already among them.

Jesus invited all men and women into the Kingdom of God. The religious leaders of his time were shocked because Jesus allowed sinners and outcasts to be his friends. They did not understand that Jesus wanted these people also to change their lives and live with him in the Kingdom. He told the religious leaders that he came to love and save all people. Even the Roman centurion was welcomed by Jesus because he showed that he had faith.

Christians say that Jesus is both God and man. The miracles show that he acted with God's power and announced God's presence on Earth. To the apostles who were with Jesus during the Transfiguration, the glory of God was revealed through Jesus. They saw Jesus' body in a radiance of light as it would appear after the Resurrection. Although the apostles were not yet really ready to understand all this, full understanding came to them after Jesus' resurrection: Jesus was God as well as man.

Christians never forget that Jesus was a man too. The Gospels tell us that he was tempted to sin by the devil, and that he cried because his friend Lazarus had died. At times Jesus was afraid and at other times he got angry. In all these ways, the Gospels remind us that Jesus was human as well as divine.

Because he was human, Jesus knew that men and women often felt that God was very far away from them. He knew that the Jewish people of his day believed God to be a judge who wanted them to obey his laws. Jesus often got angry with the Pharisees, who were strict religious leaders of the Jews, because they emphasized God's laws more than the Jews' belief that God was merciful and loving. Jesus preached that God wanted men and women to love him and to love each other.

Jesus showed the people another side of their Lord. He told them to call God "Abba," which means Father, and to pray to him by saying "Our Father." Jesus made God seem a lot closer than he had ever seemed before. He taught the people that God loved them and that God would give them what they needed as long as they asked for it in Jesus' name.

Jesus often tried to be alone so that he could pray to God. Prayer is a way of talking to God, and Jesus told his disciples that they should pray often. He taught them that prayer was something simple and natural, like a talk with a friend. He wanted them to trust and depend upon God the way boys and girls trust their parents. Jesus promised them that God would listen to them and take care of them.

It took Jesus a long time to prepare his apostles for his death. This was not something they wanted to hear about, because it frightened them. But Jesus taught them that he had to suffer so that people would be free. He tried to make them understand that he was not a warrior Messiah, but the suffering Messiah who came to lay down his life to save his people.

from the
BOOKS OF
MATTHEW, MARK,
LUKE, and JOHN

JESUS PREACHES ON FORGIVENESS

THE scribes and the Pharisees brought to him a woman caught doing wrong, and when they had placed her before him, they said, "Master, this woman was caught doing wrong, in the very act. Now Moses in the law commanded that such a person should be stoned. But what do you say?" This they said to test him, that they might be able to accuse him.

Jesus stooped down and with his finger wrote on the ground as though he had not heard them. When they continued asking him, he stood up and said to them, "He that is without sin among you, let him first cast a stone at her." And again he stooped down and wrote on the ground.

When they heard it, they went away one by one, beginning with the eldest, and Jesus was left alone, except for the woman. Then Jesus stood up and seeing no one but the woman said to her, "Woman, where are your accusers? Has no man condemned you?" She said, "No man, Lord." And Jesus said to her, "Neither do I condemn you. Go, and sin no more."

One of the Pharisees asked Jesus to eat with him. And he went into the Pharisee's house and sat down to dinner. Now there was a woman in the city who was a sinner, and when she learned that Jesus was having dinner at the Pharisee's house, she brought an alabaster box of ointment and stayed at his feet, behind him, weeping. She began to wash his feet with tears, and wipe them with the hair of her head, and kissed his feet and anointed them with ointment.

When the Pharisee who had invited him saw this, he said to himself, "This man, if he were a prophet, would have known who and what kind of woman this is who touches him, for she is a sinner." Jesus answering said to him, "Simon, I have something to say to you." And he said, "Master, speak on."

"There was a certain creditor which had two debtors. One owed him much, and the other a little. When they had nothing to pay, he forgave them both freely. Tell me then, which of them will love him most?"

"I suppose the one to whom he forgave the most," Simon said. And Jesus said to him, "You have judged rightly." Then turning to the woman, he said to Simon, "Do you see this woman? I came into your house, and you gave me no water for my feet, but she has washed my feet with tears and wiped them with the hairs of her head. You gave me no kiss, but this woman, since the moment I came in, has not stopped kissing my feet. You did not anoint my head with oil, but this woman has anointed my feet with ointment.

"Therefore, I say to you, her sins, which are many, are forgiven, for she loved much. But he to whom little is forgiven, loves little."

And he said to her, "Your sins are forgiven."

Then they that sat at dinner with him began to say within themselves, "Who is this that forgives sins also?"

And he said to the woman, "Your faith has saved you. Go in peace."

Then a man possessed with a devil, blind and dumb, was brought, and Jesus healed him so that he both spoke and saw. And all the people were amazed and said, "Is this not the Son of David?" But when the Pharisees heard it, they said, "This fellow casts out devils only through Beelzebub the prince of the devils."

Jesus knew their thoughts and said to them: "Every kingdom divided against itself is brought to ruin, and every city or house divided against itself cannot stand. If Satan casts out Satan, he is divided against himself. How then shall his kingdom stand?

"If I cast out devils through Beelzebub, through whom do your children cast them out? Therefore, they shall be your judges. But if I cast out devils through the spirit of God, then the kingdom of God has come to you. Or else, how can one enter a strong man's house and plunder his goods, unless he first tie up the strong man? Then he will plunder his house. He that is not with me is against me, and he that does not gather with me scatters.

"Therefore I say to you, all manner of sin and blasphemy shall be forgiven men, but blasphemy against the Holy Spirit shall not be forgiven men. Whoever speaks a word against the Son of man shall be forgiven, but whoever speaks against the Holy Spirit shall not be forgiven, neither in this world nor in the world to come. Every idle word that men shall speak, they shall give account of in the day of judgment. For by your words you shall be justified, and by your words you shall be condemned."

Then certain of the scribes and Pharisees said, "Master, we wish to see a sign from you." But he answered:

"An evil and indulgent generation seeks a sign, but there shall be no sign given to it except the sign of the prophet Jonah: As Jonah was three days and three nights in the whale's belly, so shall the Son of man be three days and three nights in the heart of the earth."

JESUS
PREACHES
IN PARABLES

T came to pass that he went throughout every village and city, preaching and showing the glad tidings of the kingdom of God. The twelve apostles were with him, and certain women which had been healed of evil spirits and sicknesses: Mary called Magdalene, out of whom went seven devils, and Joanna the wife of Chuza, Herod's steward, and Susanna, and many others, who cared for him out of their means.

By the seaside, great multitudes were gathered together about him, so he went into a boat and addressed the multitude who stood on the shore.

THE SOWER

And he spoke many things to them in parables, saying:

"A sower went out to sow his seed. And as he sowed, some fell by the wayside, and the fowls came and ate them up. Some fell on stony places where they had not much earth. And when the sun rose they were scorched, and because they had no root, they withered away. And some fell among thorns, and the thorns sprung up and choked them. But others fell into good ground and brought forth fruit, some a hundredfold, some sixtyfold, some thirtyfold."

And when he had said these things, he cried, "He that has ears to hear, let him hear." Then his disciples asked him, saying, "What does this parable mean?" And he said:

"To you is given to know the mysteries of the kingdom of God, but to the others I speak in parables, that seeing they still may not see, and hearing they still may not understand. Now the meaning of the parable is this:

"The seed is the word of God. Those by the wayside are they who hear. Then the devil comes and takes away the word out of their hearts, lest they should believe and be saved.

"Those on the rock are they who, when they hear, receive the word with joy, and having no roots, they believe for a while, but in time of temptation fall away.

"Those which fell among thorns are they who, when they have heard, go forth and are choked with the cares and riches and pleasures of this life, so that their faith never ripens.

"But the seed on the good ground are they who, with honest and good hearts, having heard the word, keep it and bring forth fruit with patience."

THE GRAIN OF MUSTARD SEED

He put forth another parable to them, saying:

"The kingdom of heaven is like a grain of mustard seed, which a man took and sowed in the field. It is indeed the least of all seeds, but when it is grown it is the greatest among plants, and becomes a tree, so that the birds of the air come and build nests in its branches."

THE TARES

Another parable he gave to them, saying:

"The kingdom of heaven is like a man who sowed good seed in his field, but while he slept, his enemy came and sowed tares among the wheat, and went his way. So when the blades sprung up and brought forth fruit, the tares appeared also.

"So the servants of the man came and said to him, 'Did you not sow good seed in the field? From where then have come the tares?'

" 'An enemy has done this,' he said to them, and the servants asked, 'Do you wish then that we go and gather them up?' But he said, 'No, lest while you gather up the tares, you root up the wheat with them also. Let both grow together until the harvest, and in the time of harvest, I will say to the reapers, "Gather together first the tares and bind them in bundles to burn them. But gather the wheat into my barn." ' "

THE MEANING OF THE TARES

All these things Jesus spoke to the multitude in parables. He did not speak to them without a parable, so that it might be fulfilled which was spoken by the prophet, saying:

"I will open my mouth in parables. I will utter things which have been kept secret since the foundation of the world."

Then Jesus sent the multitude away and went into a house, and his disciples came to him, saying, "Explain to us the parable of the tares of the field."

And when they were alone together, he answered:

"He that sows the good seed is the Son of man. The field is the world; the good seed are the children of the kingdom. But the tares are the children of the wicked one. The enemy that sowed them is the devil. The harvest is the end of the world; the reapers are the angels. Therefore, as the tares are gathered and burned in the fire, so shall it be at the end of the world.

"The Son of man shall send forth his angels, and they shall gather out of his kingdom all things that offend, and those who do evil, and they shall throw them into a furnace of fire. There shall be a wailing and a gnashing of teeth. Then the righteous shall shine forth like the sun in the kingdom of their Father. Who has ears to hear, let him hear."

THE NET OF FISH

"Again, the kingdom of heaven is like a net that was cast into the sea and gathered all kinds of fish. When it was full, they drew it to shore and sat down and put the good into vessels, but cast the bad away.

"So it shall be at the end of the world. The angels shall come forth and separate the wicked from the just and shall cast them into the furnace."

JESUS IN NAZARETH

WHEN Jesus had finished these parables, he departed and went into his own country, to Nazareth where he had been brought up. And as his custom was he went into the synagogue on the sabbath day, and stood up to read. The book of the prophet Isaiah was given to him, and when he opened the book, he found the place where it was written:

"The Spirit of the Lord is upon me, because he has anointed me to preach the gospel of the poor.

"He has sent me to heal the broken-hearted, to preach deliverance to the captives, and recovering of sight to the blind, to set at liberty those who are oppressed, and to preach the acceptable year of the Lord."

He closed the book and gave it back to the minister and sat down. And the eyes of all them that were in the synagogue were fastened on him. And he began to say to them, "To-day this Scripture is fulfilled in your ears."

All wondered at the gracious words that came from him, and they said, "Is this not Joseph's son? Is this not the carpenter, the son of Mary, the brother of James and Joseph, and of Jude and Simon? And are not his sisters here with us?" And they took offense at him.

But Jesus said to them, "A prophet is not without honor except in his own country and among his own kin, and in his own house."

And he marveled because of their unbelief.

And all those in the synagogue, when they heard these things, were filled with wrath, and rose up and thrust him out of the city, and led him up to the edge of the hill on which their city was built, that they might throw him down.

But he, passing through the midst of them, went his way.

JESUS CALMS THE STORM

Now it came to pass on a certain day that he went into a boat with his disciples, and said to them, "Let us go over to the other side of the lake." So they set sail. But as they sailed, he fell asleep, and there came down a storm of wind on the lake, and the boat was filled with water, so that they were in danger. The disciples awoke him saying, "Master, Master, we are sinking."

Then Jesus arose and rebuked the wind and the raging of the water, and they ceased and there was a calm. And he said to the disciples, "Where is your faith?"

They were frightened, and wondered at this, saying to one another, "What manner of man is this? For he commands even the winds and the water and they obey him."

And they came to the other side of the lake, into the country of the Gadarenes. When Jesus stepped forth on the land, he met a certain man who had had devils a long time, and wore no clothes, nor lived in any house, but had his dwelling among the tombs.

When the man saw Jesus, he cried out, and fell down before him, and with a loud voice said, "What have I done to you, Jesus, Son of God most high? I beg you, do not torment me." (For Jesus had commanded the unclean spirit to come out of the man, for often it had seized him, and though he had been kept bound with chains and in fetters, he broke the bonds and was driven by the devil into the wilderness).

"What is your name?" Jesus asked him. And he said, "Legion," because many devils were within him. And he begged Jesus not to command them to go out of the country.

Now there was a herd of many swine feeding on the mountain, and he begged him to let them enter into the swine. He allowed them, and the devils went out of the man and entered into the swine, and the herd ran violently down a steep slope into the lake, and were drowned.

When they that fed the swine saw what was done, they fled, and went and told it in the city and in the country. Then people went out to see what was done. They came to Jesus and found the man, out of whom the devils had departed, sitting at the feet of Jesus, clothed, and in his right mind. And they were afraid.

Those who had seen it told them by what means he that was possessed of the devils was healed. Then the whole multitude of the country of the Gadarenes begged Jesus to depart from them, for they were taken with great fear. So he went back into the boat. Then the man out of whom the devils were departed asked that he might go with him, but Jesus sent him away, saying, "Return to your own house, and show what great things God has done to you." So he went his way and told throughout the whole city what great things Jesus had done to him. And people marveled greatly.

JESUS RESTORES JAIRUS' DAUGHTER TO LIFE

When Jesus had returned again by boat to the other side of the lake, many people gathered about him while he was by the water. There came to him one of the rulers of the synagogue, Jairus by name. When he saw Jesus, he fell at his feet, and pleaded greatly saying, "My little daughter lies at the point of death. I pray you, come and lay your hands on her, that she

may be healed, and she shall live." Jesus went with him, and many people followed and thronged about him.

On the way, there was a woman who had suffered a flow of blood twelve years, and had been treated many times by physicians. She had spent all that she had, and was no better but had grown worse. She had heard of Jesus and came in the crowd behind him and touched his garment. For she said, "If I may only touch his clothes, I shall be well."

Immediately, the bleeding ceased and she felt in her body that she was healed. Then Jesus, feeling instantly that virtue had gone forth from him, turned around in the crowd, and said, "Who touched my clothes?"

His disciples said to him, "You see the multitude thronging about you, and do you say, 'Who touched me?' "

He looked round about to see her who had done this thing. Then the woman, fearing and trembling, knowing what was done in her, came and

And he allowed no man to follow him, except Peter, and James, and John, the brother of James. And he went to the house of the ruler of the synagogue. He saw there many weeping and wailing greatly, and when he had gone in, he said to them, "Why do you make this noise and weep? The girl is not dead, but sleeps."

They laughed at him. But when he had put them all out, he took the father and the mother of the girl, and those that were with him, and went in where

fell down before him, and told him all the truth. And he said to her, "Daughter, your faith has made you whole. Go in peace, and be healed of your plague."

While he was still speaking, there came from the ruler of the synagogue's house some men who said to Jairus, "Your daughter is dead, why trouble the Master any further?" But as soon as Jesus heard this, he said to the ruler of the synagogue, "Be not afraid. Only believe."

the girl was lying. Then he took the girl by the hand and said to her, "Talitha cumi," which means, being interpreted, "Little girl, I say to you, arise."

Immediately the girl arose, and walked—for she was twelve years old —and they were filled with great astonishment.

But he told them strictly that no man should know of it, and commanded that she should be given something to eat.

THE BEHEADING OF JOHN THE BAPTIST

NOW Herod the tetrarch heard of all that was done by Jesus, and he was perplexed, because some said that it was John the Baptist, risen from the dead. Some said that Elijah had appeared, and others that one of the old prophets had risen again. But when Herod heard of these things, he said, "It is John, whom I beheaded. He has risen from the dead."

For Herod himself had had John put in prison, for the sake of Herodias, his brother Philip's wife, whom he had married. John had said to Herod, "It is not lawful for you to have your brother's wife." Therefore Herodias had a quarrel against him. She would have had him killed, but she could not. For Herod feared John, knowing that he was a just and holy man.

But on his birthday, Herod gave a supper for his lords, high captains, and the leading men of Galilee, and the daughter of Herodias came and danced, and pleased Herod and those who sat with him. And the king said to the girl, "Ask of me whatever you will, and I will give it to you." He swore to her, "Whatever you ask of me, I will give it to you, up to half of my kingdom."

The girl went forth and said to her mother, "What shall I ask?" And her mother said, "The head of John the Baptist."

So she went directly to the king and said, "My wish is that you give me in due course, on a platter, the head of John the Baptist."

Then the king was very sorry, but because of his oath and those who sat with him, he could not reject her demand. So immediately the king sent an executioner and commanded that John's head be brought. And the executioner went and beheaded him in the prison, and brought his head on a platter, and gave it to the girl. And the girl gave it to her mother.

When his disciples heard of it, they came and took his body and laid it in a tomb, and went and told Jesus. When Jesus heard of it, he went by boat out into a deserted place, with his apostles.

THE FEEDING OF THE MULTITUDE

THE people saw them departing, and many knew him, and ran on foot from all cities, and were there before them. And Jesus, when he arrived, saw many people and was moved with compassion toward them, because they were like sheep not having a shepherd. And he began to teach them many things.

Now later in the day his disciples came to him and said, "This is a deserted place, and it is late. Send them away, so that they may go into the country round about, and into the villages, and buy themselves bread. For they have nothing to eat."

He answered and said to them, "Give them something to eat." And they said to him, "Shall we go and buy two hundred pennyworth of bread, and give it to them to eat?"

"How many loaves do you have?" he answered, "Go and see."

One of his disciples, Andrew, Simon Peter's brother, said to him, "There is a lad here who has five barley loaves and two small fishes. But what are they among so many?"

Jesus said, "Make the men sit down." Now there was much grass in the place, so the men sat down, in number about five thousand. And Jesus took the loaves, and when he had given thanks, he distributed them to the disciples, and the disciples to

those who were sitting. They did likewise with the fishes.

When they were filled, he said to his disciples, "Gather up the pieces that remain, so that nothing is lost."

Therefore, they gathered them together, and filled twelve baskets with the leftovers of the five barley loaves, which remained over and above to those who had eaten.

JESUS WALKS ON THE WATER

Jesus sent the multitudes away, and asked his disciples to get into a boat and to go ahead of him to the other side of the lake toward Capernaum. Then he went up into a mountain to pray, and when the evening came, he was there alone.

But the boat was now in the midst of the sea, tossed by the waves, for the wind was against them. And in the fourth watch of the night, Jesus went to them, walking on the sea.

When the disciples saw him walking on the sea, they were troubled and said, "It is a spirit." And they cried out for fear. But Jesus spoke to them, saying, "Be of good cheer. It is I. Be not afraid."

Peter answered him and said, "Lord, if it is you, let me come to you on the water."

"Come," he said. And Peter came down out of the boat, and he walked on the water, to go to Jesus. But when he saw the strong wind, he was afraid and began to sink. "Lord, save me," he cried, and immediately Jesus stretched forth his hand and caught him, and said to him, "O you of little faith, why did you doubt?"

And when they had come into the boat, the wind ceased. Then they that were in the boat worshiped him, saying, "Truly you are the Son of God."

JESUS QUOTES ISAIAH

When they had crossed the water, they came into the land of Gennesaret, and when the men of that place learned of him, they brought to him all that were diseased, and asked that they might only touch the hem of his garment. And as many as touched it were made perfectly well.

Then scribes and Pharisees from Jerusalem came to Jesus, saying, "Why

do your disciples revolt against the tradition of the elders? They do not wash their hands when they eat bread."

He answered and said, "You hypocrites! Well did Isaiah prophesy of you, saying:

" 'This people honors me with their lips, but their heart is far from me. And in vain do they worship me, teaching for doctrines the commandments of men.' For, laying aside the commandments of God, you hold to the tradition of men, attending to such little things as the washing of pots and cups."

Then he called the multitude and said to them, "Hear, and understand. Not that which goes into the mouth, but that which comes out of the mouth, does harm to a man."

Then his disciples came and said to him, "Did you know that the Pharisees were offended after they heard this saying?" But he answered and said:

"Every plant which my heavenly Father has not planted shall be rooted up. Let them alone. They are blind leaders of the blind. And if the blind lead the blind, both shall fall into the ditch."

"Explain to us this parable," Peter said to him. And Jesus said:

"Are you also still without understanding? Do you still not understand that whatever goes in at the mouth goes only into the belly. But those things which come out of the mouth come forth from the heart, and they defile a man. For out of the heart come evil thoughts, murders, wrongdoing, thefts, blasphemies, false witness. These are the things which defile a man. But to eat with unwashed hands defiles no one."

From there, Jesus went into Tyre and Sidon. Then he returned to the sea of Galilee, through the region of the Decapolis. Next he came in a ship to

Dalmanutha, then to Bethsaida. In all these places he preached and healed.

And when Jesus came into the coasts of Caesarea Philippi, he asked his disciples, "Who do men say that I, the Son of man, am?" And they said, "Some say you are John the Baptist, some, Elijah, and others, Jeremiah or one of the prophets."

"But who do you say that I am?" he asked. And Simon Peter answered and said, "You are the Christ, the Son of the living God."

Jesus said to him, "Blessed are you, Simon, son of Jonah, for flesh and blood have not revealed it to you, but my Father who is in heaven.

"And I say also to you that you are Peter, the rock, and upon this rock I will build my church. And the gates of hell shall not prevail against it. I will give to you the keys of the kingdom of heaven, and whatever you bind on earth shall be bound in heaven, and whatever you loose on earth shall be loosed in heaven." Then he told his disciples that they should tell no man that he was Jesus the Christ.

JESUS FORETELLS
THE CRUCIFIXION

From that time forth, Jesus began to tell his disciples how he must go to Jerusalem, and suffer many things from the elders and chief priests and scribes, and be killed, and be raised again the third day. Then Peter began to rebuke him, saying, "Be it far from true, Lord. This shall not happen to you."

But he turned and said to Peter: "Get thee behind me, Satan. You are an offense to me, for you are not concerned with the things of God, but those of men."

Then Jesus said to his disciples:

"If any man wishes to come after me, let him deny himself and take up his cross and follow me. For whoever wishes to save his life, shall lose it, and whoever will lose his life for my sake shall find it. For what shall it profit a man if he shall gain the whole world and lose his own soul? Or what shall a man give in exchange for his soul? Whoever therefore shall be ashamed of me and of my words in this indulgent and sinful generation, of him also shall the Son of man be ashamed, when he comes in the glory of his Father with the holy angels, to reward every man according to his works."

And he said to them, "Truly I say to you that there are some of them that stand here who shall not taste of death till they have seen the kingdom of God come with power."

THE TRANSFIGURATION

After six days, Jesus took Peter, James, and John his brother and brought them up into a high mountain, and was transfigured before them: his face shone like the sun and his clothing was as white as light. And, behold, there appeared to them Moses and Elijah talking with him.

Then Peter said, "Lord, it is good for us to be here. If you will, let us make three tabernacles here, one for you, one for Moses, and one for Elijah."

While he still spoke, behold, a bright cloud overshadowed them, and a voice came out of the cloud, saying: "This is my beloved Son, in whom I am well pleased. Listen to him." And when the disciples heard it, they fell on their faces and were much afraid.

But Jesus came and touched them, and said: "Arise and do not be afraid." And when they had lifted up their eyes, they saw no man, except Jesus alone.

As they came down the mountain, Jesus commanded them, saying, "Tell

the vision to no man, until the Son of man has risen again from the dead." And his disciples asked him, saying, "Why then do the scribes say that Elijah must come first?"

Jesus answered, "Elijah truly must come first and restore all things. But I say to you, that Elijah has come already, and they did not know him, but have done to him whatever they pleased. Likewise shall the Son of man also suffer from them."

Then the disciples understood that he spoke to them of John the Baptist.

JESUS INSTRUCTS THE DISCIPLES

 O N the next day, when they had come down from the mountain, many people met them. And a man in the crowd cried out, "Master, I beg you, look at my son, for he is my only child. A spirit has taken him and at times he cries out suddenly and often he falls into the fire, and often into the water. I brought him to your disciples, but they could not cure him."

Then Jesus answered and said, "O faithless and perverse generation, how long shall I be with you? How long shall I bear you? Bring him here to me." And Jesus rebuked the devil, and he departed out of him, and the child was cured from that very hour.

Then the disciples came to Jesus privately and said, "Why could we not cast it out?" And Jesus said to them, "Because of your unbelief. For truly I say to you, if you have faith as small as a grain of mustard seed, you shall say to this mountain, 'Move hence to yonder place,' and it shall move, and nothing shall be impossible to you. However, this happens only by prayer and fasting."

They departed and passed through Galilee, and Jesus taught his disciples, saying, "The Son of man shall be delivered into the hands of men, and they shall kill him, and after he is killed, he shall rise the third day." But they did not understand his words, and were afraid to ask him.

And he came to Capernaum, and in a house he asked them, "What was it you disputed among yourselves on the way?" But they held their silence, since on the way they had disputed among themselves about who should be the greatest.

Then Jesus sat down and called the twelve, and said to them, "If any man desires to be first, he must be last of all, and servant of all." And he took a child and placed him in the midst of them and, taking him in his arms, he said, "Whoever shall receive

one such child in my name, receives me. And whoever receives me, receives not me, but him that sent me."

Then John said, "Master, we saw someone casting out devils in your name, and we forbade him, because he does not follow us." But Jesus said, "Do not forbid him, for there is no man that does a miracle in my name that can easily speak evil of me. For he that is not against us is for us. Whoever shall give you a cup of water to drink in my name, because you belong to Christ, truly I say to you, he shall not lose his reward.

"And whoever shall offend one of these little ones that believe in me, it is better for him that a millstone were hanged around his neck, and he were cast into the sea.

"And if your hand offends you, cut it off. It is better for you to enter into life maimed than to have two hands to go into hell, into the fire that shall never be put out. And if your foot causes you to sin, cut it off. It is better for you to enter lame into life than having two feet to be cast into hell. And if your eye offends you, pluck it out. It is better for you to enter into the kingdom of God with one eye, than having two eyes to be cast into hell.

"Moreover, if your brother trespasses against you, go and tell him his fault between you and him alone. If he shall hear you, you have gained your brother. But if he will not hear you, then take with you one or two witnesses, so that every word may be established. And if he will not hear them, tell it to the church. But if he refuses to hear the church, let him be like a heathen and a publican to you.

"I say to you that if two of you agree on earth concerning anything that they shall ask, it shall be done for them by my Father who is in heaven. For where two or three are gathered together in my name, there am I in the midst of them."

THE PARABLE OF THE UNMERCIFUL SERVANT

Then Peter came to him and said, "Lord, how often shall my brother sin against me, and I forgive him? Up to seven times?"

Jesus said to him, "I say to you, not seven times, but seventy times seven.

"Thus the kingdom of heaven is like a certain king who had a servant that owed him ten thousand talents. Because he could not pay, his lord ordered him to be sold, and his wife and children and all that he had, and payment be made. The servant there-fore fell down and worshiped him, saying, 'Lord, have patience with me, and I will pay you all.' Then the lord of that servant was moved with compassion and freed him and forgave him the debt.

"But the same servant went out and found one of his fellow servants who owed him a hundred pence, and he laid hands on him, and took him by the throat, saying, 'Pay me what you owe.' And his fellow servant fell down at his feet and begged him, saying, 'Have patience with me, and I will pay you all.' And he would not, but went and cast him into prison, till he should pay the debt.

"So when his fellow servants saw what was done, they were very sorry, and came and told to their lord all that was done.

"Then his lord, after calling him forth, said to him, 'O wicked servant, I forgave you all that debt, because you begged me. Should you not also have had compassion on your fellow servant, even as I had pity on you?' And his lord was angered and delivered him to the torturers, till he should pay all that was due to him. So likewise shall my heavenly Father do also to you, if you do not forgive from your hearts your brothers' trespasses."

It came to pass that when Jesus had finished these sayings, he departed from Galilee and came into the coasts of Judea beyond the Jordan. And great multitudes followed him, and he healed them there.

As he went along the road, a certain man said to him, "Lord I will follow you wherever you go." Jesus said to him, "Foxes have holes and birds of the air have nests, but the Son of man has nowhere to lay his head."

He said to another, "Follow me." But the man said, "Lord, allow me first to go and bury my father." Jesus said to him, 'Let the dead bury their dead, but you go and preach the kingdom of God."

And another said, "Lord, I will follow you, but let me first go bid them farewell who are at my home." And Jesus said to him, "No man, having put his hand to the plough, who looks back, is fit for the kingdom of God."

SEVENTY MORE DISCIPLES ARE APPOINTED

After these things, Jesus appointed seventy more disciples and sent them two by two ahead of him into every city and place where he himself would come. And he said to them:

"The harvest truly is great, but the laborers are few. Pray, therefore, to the Lord of the harvest, to send forth laborers into his harvest.

"Go your ways. Behold, I send you forth as lambs among wolves. Carry neither purse, nor money, nor shoes, and salute no man along the way. And into whatever house you enter, first say, 'Peace be to this house.'

"And remain in the same house, eating and drinking such things as they give, for the laborer is worthy of his hire. Do not go from house to house.

"Into whatever city you enter, and they receive you, eat such things as are set before you, and heal the sick that are therein, and say to them, 'The kingdom of God is near.' But whatever city you enter that receives you not, go your ways out into the streets of the same, and say, 'Even the very dust of your city, which clings to us, we wipe off against you. Nevertheless, be sure of this, that the kingdom of God is near.' But I say to you that it shall be more tolerable in that day for Sodom than for that city.

"He that hears you, hears me, and he that despises you, despises me, and he that despises me, despises him that sent me."

THE GOOD SAMARITAN

A certain lawyer stood up and tested him, saying, "Master, what shall I do to inherit eternal life?" Jesus answered, "What is written in the law? How do you read it?"

The lawyer said, "You shall love the Lord your God with all your heart, and with all your soul, and with all your strength, and with all your mind, and your neighbor as yourself."

And Jesus said to him, "You have answered right. Do this, and you shall live." But the lawyer, wishing to justify himself, said to Jesus, "And who is my neighbor?" And Jesus answering said:

"A certain man went down from Jerusalem to Jericho and fell among thieves who stripped him of his clothing, and wounded him, and departed, leaving him for dead. And by chance there came a certain priest that way, and when he saw him, he passed by on the other side. And likewise a Levite, when he was at the place, came and looked at him, and passed by on the other side.

"But a certain Samaritan, as he journeyed, came where he was, and when he saw him, he had compassion on him. He went to him and bound up his wounds, pouring on oil and wine, and put him on his own beast, and brought him to an inn and took care of him.

"And the next day, when he departed, he gave some money to the innkeeper and said to him, 'Take care of him, and whatever more you spend, when I come again, I will repay you.'

"Now which of these three, do you think, was a neighbor to him that fell among the thieves?"

And the lawyer said, "He that showed mercy on him." Then Jesus said to him, "Go, and do likewise."

THE RICH YOUNG RULER

A certain ruler asked him, saying also, "Good Master, what shall I do to inherit eternal life?" And Jesus said to him, "Why do you call me good? There is none good but one, that is, God. You know the commandments: Do not commit adultery. Do not kill. Do not steal. Do not bear false witness. Honor thy father and mother."

And he answered and said to Jesus, "Master, all these things I have observed from my youth." Then Jesus looking at him, loved him, and said to him, "One thing you lack: Go your way, sell whatever you have, and give to the poor, and you shall have treasure in heaven. Then come, take up the cross, and follow me."

The young man was sad at these words, and went away grieved. For he had great possessions.

And Jesus looked round about, and said to his disciples, "How hard it shall be for them that have riches to enter into the kingdom of God!" The disciples were astonished at his words, but Jesus answered again and said to them, "Children, how hard it is for them that trust in riches to enter into the kingdom of God! It is easier for a camel to go through the eye of a needle than for a rich man to enter into the kingdom of God."

They were astonished beyond measure, and said among themselves, "Who then can be saved?" And Jesus looking upon them said, "With men it is impossible, but not with God. For with God all things are possible."

Then Peter said, "Behold, we have foresaken all and followed you. What shall we have therefore?" And Jesus said to them:

"Truly I say to you which have followed me that, in the day when the Son of man shall sit in the throne of his glory, you also shall sit upon twelve thrones, judging the twelve tribes of Israel. And everyone that has forsaken houses, or brothers, or sisters, or father, or mother, or wife, or children, or lands, for my name's sake, shall receive a hundredfold, and shall inherit everlasting life.

"But many that are first shall be last, and the last shall be first.

THE LABORERS IN THE VINEYARD

"For the kingdom of heaven is like an householder who went out early in the morning to hire laborers for his vineyard. When he had agreed with his laborers on a silver piece a day, he sent them into his vineyard.

"He went out about nine o'clock and saw others standing idle in the market place; and said to them, 'Go to my vineyard too, and whatever is right I will give you.' And they went their way. He went out about noon and again at mid-afternoon, and did likewise. And near the end of the day he went out, and found others standing idle, and said to them, 'Why do you stand here idle?' They said to him, 'Because no one has hired us.' He said to them, 'Go to my vineyard, too, and whatever is right, you will receive.'

"So when evening came, the lord of the vineyards said to his steward, 'Call the laborers and give them their wages, beginning from the last to the first.'

"And when those came who were hired near the end of the day, each one received a silver piece. So when the first came, they supposed that they would receive more; but they likewise each received a silver piece.

"When they had received it, they murmured against the man of the house, saying, 'These last have worked only one hour, and you have made them equal to us who have borne the burden and heat of the day.' But he answered one of them, and said, 'Friend, I do you no wrong. Did you not agree with me on a silver piece? Take what is yours and go your way. I will give to the last the same as to you. Is it not lawful for me to do what I will with what is mine? Is your eye greedy, because I am generous?'

"So the last shall be first, and the first last."

JOY IN HEAVEN

All the publicans and sinners drew near to Jesus to hear him. And the Pharisees and scribes murmured, saying, "This man receives sinners and eats with them." Then Jesus spoke this parable to them, saying:

"What man of you, having a hundred sheep, if he loses one of them, does not leave the ninety and nine in the wilderness, and go after that which is lost, until he finds it? And when he has found it, he lays it on his shoulders, rejoicing. And when he comes home, he calls together his friends and neighbors, saying to them, 'Rejoice with me, for I have found my sheep which was lost.' I say to you that likewise there shall be more joy in heaven over one sinner that repents than over ninety and nine just persons who need no repentance.

"Or what woman, if she has ten pieces of silver and loses one, does not light a candle and sweep the house and seek diligently till she finds it?

And when she has found it, she calls her friends and her neighbors together, saying, 'Rejoice with me, for I have found the piece which I had lost.' Likewise, I say to you, there is joy in the presence of the angels of God over one sinner who repents."

THE PRODIGAL SON

And Jesus said:

"A certain man had two sons. The younger of them said to his father, 'Father, give me the portion of goods that I will inherit.' So he divided his property between them. And not many days after, the younger son gathered all together and took a journey into a far country, and there wasted his wealth in riotous living. And when he had spent all, there arose a mighty famine in that land, and he began to be in want. So he went and hired himself out to a citizen of that country, who sent him into his fields to feed pigs. He was ready to fill himself with the husks the pigs ate, for no man gave

him anything. When he came to himself, he said, 'How many hired servants of my father's have bread enough and to spare, while I am perishing with hunger. I will arise and go to my father, and will say to him, 'Father, I have sinned against heaven and before you. I am not worthy any more to be called your son. Make me one of your hired servants.'

"He rose up and went to his father. But when he was still a long way off, his father saw him, and had pity; and ran and fell on his neck and kissed him. The son said to him: 'Father, I have sinned against heaven, and in your eyes, and am no longer worthy to be called your son.'

"But the father said to his servants, 'Bring out the best robe, and put it on him. And put a ring on his hand, and shoes on his feet. And bring out the fatted calf and kill it, and let us eat and be merry. For this son of mine was dead, and is alive again. He was lost and is found.'

And they began to be merry.

"Now his elder son was in the field. And as he came and drew near the house, he heard music and dancing. He called one of the servants and asked what these things meant. He said to him, 'Your brother has come home. And your father has killed the fatted calf because he has him back, safe and sound.'

"He was angry, and would not go in. So his father came out and pleaded with him. He answered his father, saying, 'Lo, these many years I have served you, never at any time disobeying any of your commandments. And yet you never gave me a kid, so that I might make merry with my friends. But as soon as this other son of yours came, who has eaten up your wealth in riotous living, you killed the fatted calf for him.'

"And the father said to him, 'Son, you are always with me, and all that I have is yours. It is fitting that we should make merry, and be glad; for this your brother was dead, and is alive again; was lost, and is found.'

THE RICH MAN AND THE BEGGAR

"There was a certain rich man, who was clothed in purple and fine linen, and dined sumptuously every day. And there was a certain beggar named Lazarus who lay at his gate, covered with sores, and desiring from the rich man's table. The dogs even came and licked his sores.

"It came to pass that the beggar died, and was carried by the angels to Abraham's side. The rich man also died, and was buried. And in hell he lifted up his eyes, being in torment; and saw Abraham afar off, and Lazarus with him.

"He cried out and said, 'Father Abraham, have mercy on me, and send Lazarus, that he may dip the tip of his finger in water, and cool my tongue. For I am tormented in this flame.'

"But Abraham said, 'Son, remember

that you in your lifetime received your good things, and Lazarus bad things; but now he is comforted and you are tormented. And besides all this, there is a great gulf set between you and us; so that those who would pass from here to you cannot; neither can they who would pass from your side come to us.'

"Then the rich man said, 'I beg you then, father, to send him to my father's house; where I have five brothers, so that he may warn them, lest they also come into this place of torment.'

"Abraham said to him, 'They have Moses and the prophets, let them listen to them.' And he said, 'No, father Abraham, but if one went to them from the dead, they would repent.'

"And Abraham said to him, 'If they do not listen to Moses and the prophets, they will not be persuaded; even though one rises from the dead.'"

THE JOURNEY TO JERUSALEM

A S Jesus was on his way to Jerusalem, he passed through the midst of Samaria and Galilee. And as he entered a certain village, there met him ten men that were lepers, who stood afar off. And they lifted up their voices and cried, "Jesus, Master, have mercy on us." And when he saw them, he said to them, "Go and show yourselves to the priests." And it came to pass that as they went they were healed. And one of them, when he saw that he was healed, turned back, and with a loud voice glorified God, and fell down on his face at his feet, giving him thanks. And he was a Samaritan.

And Jesus said, "Were there not ten healed? But where are the nine? Only this stranger has returned to give glory to God." And he said to him, "Arise, go your way; your faith has made you whole."

A PARABLE OF PRAYER

Jesus spoke this parable to certain men who were proud of their own righteousness and looked down upon others: "Two men went up into the temple to pray, the one a Pharisee, the other a tax gatherer.

"The Pharisee stood and prayed by himself in these words: 'God, I thank you that I am not like other men, greedy, unjust, indulgent, or like this tax gatherer! I fast twice in the week, and I give a tenth of all I own to charity.'

"But the publican, standing far off, would not lift up so much as his eyes to heaven, but beat upon his breast, saying, 'God be merciful to me, a sinner.'

"I tell you, this man went down to his house justified rather than the other. For everyone that exalts himself shall be humbled, and he that humbles himself shall be exalted."

JESUS PREPARES THE DISCIPLES

They were on the road going up to Jerusalem, and Jesus went before them. And as the disciples followed, they were amazed and afraid. Then he called again the twelve and began to tell them what things should happen to him, saying:

"Behold, we go up to Jerusalem. The Son of man shall be delivered to the chief priests and to the scribes, and they shall condemn him to death and shall deliver him to the Gentiles. And they shall mock him, and shall beat him, and shall spit upon him, and shall kill him. And the third day he shall rise again."

James and John, the sons of Zebedee, came to him saying, "Master, will you do for us whatever we shall desire?" He said to them, "What do you want that I should do for you?"

baptized with the baptism that I am baptized with?"

They said to him, "We can." And Jesus said to them, "You shall indeed drink of the cup that I drink of, and with the baptism that I am baptized you shall be baptized. But to sit on my right hand and on my left hand is not mine to give, but it shall be given to them for whom it has been prepared."

When the other ten heard it, they began to be much displeased with James and John. But Jesus called them to him and said to them, "You know that they which rule over the Gentiles exercise strong authority over them. But it shall not be so among

"Grant us," they said, "that we may sit, one on your right hand and the other on your left hand, in your glory."

But Jesus said to them, "You know not what you ask. Can you drink of the same cup that I drink of, and be

you: Whoever will be great among you, shall be your servant, and whoever of you will be the greatest, shall be a servant to all. For even the Son of man came not to be ministered to, but to minister, and to give his life as a ransom for many."

Jesus entered and passed through Jericho. And there was a man named Zaccheus, the chief among the tax collectors, who was rich and who tried to see Jesus, to learn who he was. But he could not because of the crowd, for he was small in size. So he ran ahead and climbed up into a sycamore tree to see him, for he was to pass that way.

When Jesus came to the place, he looked up and saw him and said to him, "Zaccheus, make haste and come down, for today I must stay at your house." And he made haste and came down, and received him joyfully.

When the people saw it, they all murmured, saying, "He has gone to be a guest with a man that is a sinner."

Then Zaccheus stood and said to the Lord, "Behold, Lord, half of my goods I give to the poor. And if I have taken anything from any man by false accusation, I repay him fourfold."

And Jesus said to him, "This day salvation has come to this house, inasmuch as he also is a son of Abraham. For the Son of man has come to seek and to save that which was lost."

JESUS AT THE HOME OF MARY AND MARTHA

Now it came to pass, as they went, that he entered into a certain village called Bethany, and a certain woman named Martha received him into her house. She had a sister called Mary, who sat at Jesus' feet and heard his word. But Martha was busy with much serving and came to him and said, "Lord, do you not care that my sister has left me to serve alone? Tell her therefore that she should help me."

Jesus answered and said to her, "Martha, Martha, you are careful and troubled about many things. But only one thing is needful. Mary has chosen that good part, which shall not be taken away from her."

LAZARUS IS RAISED FROM THE DEAD

On another occasion Lazarus, the brother of Mary, was sick. So his sisters sent word to Jesus, saying, "Lord, he whom you love is sick." For Jesus loved Martha, and her sister, and Lazarus.

When he heard therefore that he was sick, he stayed two days more in the place where he was. After that he said to his disciples, "Our friend Lazarus sleeps, but I go, that I may awake him out of sleep."

Then his disciples said, "Lord, if he sleeps, he shall be well." Then Jesus said to them plainly, "Lazarus is dead. And I am glad for your sakes that I was not there, in order that you

623

may believe. Nevertheless, let us go to him."

Then Thomas, who was called the Twin, said to his fellow disciples, "Let us go also, that we may die with him."

When Jesus came, he found that Lazarus had lain in the grave four days already. And since Bethany was close to Jerusalem, about two miles away, many of the Jews had come to Martha and Mary, to comfort them concerning their brother.

Now Martha, as soon as she heard that Jesus was coming, went and met him, but Mary sat still in the house. Martha said to Jesus, "Lord, if you had been here, my brother would not have died. But I know that even now whatever you will ask of God, God will give it to you."

rection, and the life. He that believes in me, though he is dead, shall live. And whoever lives and believes in me shall never die. Do you believe this?"

She said to him, "Yes, Lord, I believe that you are the Christ, the Son of God, which was to come into the world." And when she had so spoken she went her way, and called Mary her sister secretly, saying, "The Master has come, and calls for you." As soon as Mary heard that, she arose quickly and came to him.

Now Jesus was not yet in the town, but was in that place where Martha met him. The Jews then who had seen her in the house, and had comforted her, when they saw Mary rise up hastily and go out, followed her, saying, "She goes to the grave to weep there."

"Your brother shall rise again," said Jesus. And Martha said, "I know that he shall surely rise again in the resurrection at the last day."

Jesus said to her, "I am the resur-

When Mary had come to where Jesus was and saw him, she fell down at his feet, saying to him, "Lord, if you had been here, my brother would not have died."

When Jesus saw her weeping, and also the Jews weeping that came with her, he groaned in the spirit and was troubled, and said, "Where have you laid him?"

They said to him, "Lord, come and see." Jesus wept, and the Jews said, "Behold how much he loved him!" And some of them said, "Could not this man, who opened the eyes of the blind, have caused that Lazarus should not have died?"

Jesus therefore groaning again within himself came to the grave. It was a cave, and a stone lay upon it. Jesus said, "Take away the stone."

Then Martha said, "Lord, by this time he is decaying, for he has been dead four days." But Jesus said to her, "Did I not say to you that if you

would believe, you would see the glory of God?"

They took away the stone from the grave, and Jesus lifted up his eyes and said, "Father, I thank you for having

heard me. And I know that you hear me always, but because of the people who stand here, I said it, that they might believe that you have sent me."

And when he had thus spoken, he cried in a loud voice, "Lazarus, come forth."

And he that was dead came forth, bound hand and foot with grave clothes, and his face was bound about with a napkin. Jesus said to them, "Unbind him, and let him go."

Then many of the people who had come with Mary and had seen the things which Jesus did, believed in him. But some of them went their ways to the Pharisees, and told them what things Jesus had done.

JESUS' ENEMIES PLOT TO KILL HIM

Then the chief priests and the Pharisees held a council, and said, "What are we to do? This man does many miracles. If we let him alone, all men will believe in him, and the Romans shall come and take away both our holy place and our nation."

One of them, named Caiaphas, being the high priest that year, said to them, "You know nothing and do not realize that it is expedient for us that one man should die for the people, and that the whole nation should not perish."

This was not his own opinion, but being high priest that year, he prophesied that Jesus should die for the nation. And not for the nation only, but also that he should gather together the children of God that were scattered abroad.

From that day forth, they planned together how to put him to death.

Jesus therefore walked no longer openly among the Jews, but went into a country near the wilderness, into a city called Ephraim, and there continued with his disciples.

THE SUPPER AT BETHANY

Now the Jews' passover was near at hand, and many went out of the country up to Jerusalem before the passover, to purify themselves. There they looked for Jesus and spoke among themselves, as they stood in the temple, "What do you think? Do you believe that he will not come to the feast?" For both the chief priests and the Pharisees had given a commandment that, if any man knew where he was, he should announce it, that they might seize him.

Then Jesus six days before the passover came to Bethany, where Lazarus was whom he had raised from the dead. There they made him a supper, and Martha served. But Lazarus was one of them that sat at the table with him.

Mary took a pound of ointment of spikenard, very costly, and anointed the feet of Jesus, and wiped his feet with her hair. And the whole house was filled with the odor of the ointment.

Then said one of his disciples, Judas Iscariot, Simon's son, who was to betray him, "Why was not this ointment sold for three hundred pence, and given to the poor?" This he said, not that he cared for the poor, but because he was a thief, and had the money bag and would take what was put in it.

Then Jesus said, "Let her alone. For the day of my burying has she kept this. The poor you always have with you, but me you do not have always."

Many people knew that he was there, and they came not only for Jesus' sake, but that they might see Lazarus also, whom he had raised from the dead. But the chief priests consulted together in order that they might put Lazarus also to death, because he was the cause of many of the Jews going away from them, and believing in Jesus.

ILLUSTRATED
GLOSSARY

Alabaster box (p. 588)

Perfumes, ointments, and unguents were stored in small urns or flasks (often translated as boxes) made from alabaster, a soft marblelike stone. The flasks had many different shapes, but were usually about five inches tall and had a wide mouth.

Alabaster is a term applied to two substances: calcium carbonate and calcium sulfate. The alabaster of the New Testament was usually calcium carbonate that came from Egypt. It was a translucent milky yellow, streaked with light and dark.

Beelzebub (p. 590)

The Israelites detested the idol worship practiced by their pagan neighbors. To ridicule Baal, the god of the Canaanites, the Jews called him Beelzebub, which meant "the lord of the flies." They also used the name Beelzebub to mean "the prince of the devils," or Satan.

Bethany (p. 624)

There were two towns in Palestine named Bethany. The one where Martha, Mary, and Lazarus lived was located only two miles from Jerusalem, on the eastern slope of the Mount of Olives. Today a town named El-Azariyeh is built on the site of Bethany.

Bethsaida (p. 606)

The name Bethsaida means "house of fish," an appropriate title, for the two Bethsaidas on the Sea of Galilee were near the best fishing waters in the area. The Bethsaida mentioned here was probably the town later named Bethsaida-Julias, which was located at the northeastern end of the Sea of Galilee, near the mouth of the Jordan River. "Julias" was added to the name of Bethsaida to honor the daughter of Augustus Caesar, the Roman emperor.

Bethsaida-Julias was the birthplace of the apostles Peter, Andrew, and Philip.

Caesarea Philippi (p. 606)

Caesarea Philippi was a city built by Philip, a son of Herod the Great, on the beautiful slopes of Mount Hermon, near the source of the Jordan River. It was named in honor of Tiberius Caesar and of Philip himself.

Centuries earlier, the site of Caesarea Philippi had been sacred to the nature gods of the Canaanites. Later it was dedicated to the Greek nature god, Pan. The modern city Banias is built on the site of Caesarea Philippi, which is now part of eastern Syria.

Caiaphas (p.625)

Caiaphas was a member of the party of Sadducees, and was appointed high priest by the Roman governor in A.D. 18. As a high priest, he was chairman of the Sanhedrin, or Senate, of Palestine. The Sanhedrin had been organized some time after the Jews returned from the Babylonian exile. It was the highest court of the land, but it ruled in matters which concerned only the Jews and had no connection with the interests of the Roman government. The seventy members of the Sanhedrin met in a building near the temple in Jerusalem.

When Pontius Pilate was recalled to Rome, Caiaphas was removed from office.

Cast out devils (p. 590)

In the time of Jesus, it was believed that diseases, especially mental and nervous illnesses, were caused by the workings of evil spirits, or devils, that occupied a victim's body. When Jesus cured a person of a disease, people thought that the disease-causing devil had been cast out of the person's body.

The casting out of evil spirits is called exorcism.

Dalmanutha (p. 606)

No one knows exactly where Dalmanutha was located, but most likely it was on the western shore of the Sea of Galilee.

Decapolis (p. 605)

In the 4th century B.C., the territory east of the Jordan River and a small area west of the river was settled by Greeks. It was known as Decapolis.

In the communities of Decapolis the Greeks built pagan temples, stadiums, and theatres, like those in their homeland. The people continued to speak their own language, Greek, and soon many of their Jewish neighbors became familiar with it. Jesus is believed to have been one of those Jews who could speak Greek as well as Aramaic, the language of Palestine, Syria, and Mesopotamia.

The cities of Decapolis were almost completely self-governing, although they were supposedly under

PALESTINE DURING MINISTRY OF JESUS

0 — 30
Miles

Under Herod Antipas
Under Pontius Pilate
Under Philip
Under semi-independent rule

© Copyright 1957 by Map Projects Inc.

the rule of the province of Syria. The name Decapolis comes from the Greek and means "ten cities," but the exact number of cities that existed in that area is not known.

Deliver him to the Gentiles (p. 621)

Jesus predicted that he would be condemned to death. He said that after the condemnation, he would be handed over to the Gentiles, who would carry out the sentence. The Gentiles referred to by Jesus were the Roman authorities.

Down from Jerusalem to Jericho (p. 612)

When Luke tells us that someone went "down" to a place, he is saying that the journey was quite literally a downhill one, and not a southbound one as we frequently interpret it today. Palestine was a land of hills and valleys, and travel there was difficult.

Since Jerusalem was built on hills and Jericho was 800 feet below sea level, the road from Jerusalem to Jericho was downhill all the way. Those who traveled on it had to go up or down a steep incline. This particular road also led past rocks where robbers lurked, as the story of the good Samaritan illustrates.

Elijah must come first (p. 607)

In the Second Book of Kings, the Bible says that the prophet Elijah did not die as do other humans, but was taken up into heaven in a fiery chariot. The people believed that he would come back to prepare for the coming of the Messiah. Much later in Jewish history, a belief arose among the people that Elijah would return to earth to die like the rest of mankind.

Ephraim (p. 625)

The location of Ephraim is uncertain, but it was most likely situated in Samaria between Jericho and Bethel. There, in the dry wilderness area of Ephraim, Abraham had made camp when he first entered Canaan.

People have lived in that vicinity since around 2000 B.C. The modern town of Taiyibeh is probably built on the ancient site of Ephraim.

Fatted calf (p. 617)

The well-to-do farmers of Palestine usually kept one or more of their finest calves in stalls and fattened them with special food. These animals were intended to provide tender meat for the main dish at feasts and banquets.

The prophet Amos, who lived during the reign of Jeroboam II, king of the Northern Kingdom, seems to have had a poor opinion of this custom because he said: "Woe to those who . . . eat calves from the midst of the stall."

In general, the Jews did not eat beef. They preferred to eat the meat of sheep and goats.

Fourth watch of the night (p. 604)

In those days before the invention of clocks, the hours of the night were di-

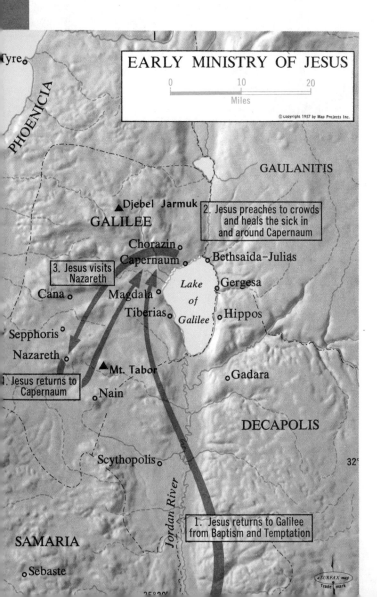

EARLY MINISTRY OF JESUS

0   10   20
Miles

© Copyright 1957 by Map Projects Inc.

Tyre

PHOENICIA

GAULANITIS

Djebel Jarmuk

GALILEE

2. Jesus preaches to crowds and heals the sick in and around Capernaum

Chorazin

Capernaum

Bethsaida–Julias

3. Jesus visits Nazareth

Cana

Magdala

Lake of Galilee

Gergesa

Tiberias

Hippos

Sepphoris

Nazareth

Mt. Tabor

Gadara

1. Jesus returns to Capernaum

Nain

DECAPOLIS

Scythopolis

32°

Jordan River

1. Jesus returns to Galilee from Baptism and Temptation

SAMARIA

Sebaste

vided into watches. The four night watches were evening, midnight, dawn, and morning. Morning was the fourth watch of the night.

Gadarenes (p. 597)

The Gadarenes were the people of the Greek city of Gadara, which was in Decapolis. (See Decapolis.) Gadara was about five miles east of the Sea of Galilee.

Gennesaret (p. 604)

The Sea of Galilee was also known as the Lake of Gennesaret or the Water of Genesar. Both of these names were derived from the name of the rich plain which lay northwest of the lake.

The Sea of Galilee was also known as Lake Tiberias, in honor of the Roman emperor of that name. In very ancient times, it had also been called the Sea of Chinnereth.

Herodias (p. 600)

Herodias had been the wife of Philip, son of Herod the Great, but she left him and married his half brother Herod Antipas. The law of Moses forbade a man to marry his brother's wife while his brother was still alive. By openly breaking the law, Herod Antipas showed his disregard for the feelings of the Jewish people.

John the Baptist, acting like the prophets of old, reprimanded Herod and Herodias for their wrongdoing, and he was killed for this act of courage.

A Hundredfold (p. 614)

To receive something back a hundredfold means to receive one hundred times the amount that was originally given.

The Lost piece of silver (p. 616)

When a Jewish woman was married, her family gave her pieces of silver or coins. Such coins were sewn into the veil she would wear as a head covering in the coming years. A poor family could give only a few coins, and they were then valued even more.

The parable of the lost coin may be telling about such a lost memento, and if so, the woman's distress is understandable. To a poor woman, the loss of even a coin of small value was important. But even more, she would have mourned the loss because the coin was a gift from her family.

Mustard (p. 594)

Mustard is an herb with yellow flowers. The mustard grown in biblical times could reach a height of twelve feet or more. Its pungent seeds are very small and were used to flavor foods.

Today mustard seeds are ground into a powder and mixed with water, vinegar, and spices to make the condiment we call mustard. In the United States mustard plants are grown in fields by farmers, and are also found growing in the wild. The mustard plant of North America grows only to about two feet.

Ointment of spikenard (p. 626)

Ointments and salves were widely used in Palestine to prevent or treat sunburn, to keep insects off the skin, and for other medicinal purposes. The most valued ointments were fragrant, but such ointments were quite costly, for they had to be brought by caravan or ship from distant lands. Only the wealthy could afford them.

Spikenard is believed to have been an Asian plant whose stems and roots had a pleasant odor. These plant parts were mixed into a salve to make a fragrant ointment. The ointment was packed into alabaster boxes to preserve it.

Parable (p.592)

A parable is an invented story that is told to teach people a spiritual or moral lesson.

The Portion of goods that I will inherit (p. 616)

The young man who was the prodigal son of this parable had no legal right to ask his father to give him the property he would inherit upon his father's death. And even though the father had put the money into his young son's hands, the boy had no right to use it without his father's permission. This was the law. But if a father turned property over to his sons, the father still had the right to any profit it might earn, and he could legally demand interest on that money.

Prodigal (p.616)

Prodigal means extravagant, or overly generous with money. The younger son in the parable is described as prodigal because he wasted his money "in riotous living."

Prophet (p. 588)

As it is used here, the word prophet means a seer, one who obtains information intuitively, without learning it from outside sources. Today such people are called psychics.

Samaritans (p. 613)

When the Ten Tribes of Israel were exiled from their homeland, some Israelites were left to live among the pagan captives that the Assyrians had brought to live in the almost empty land of Israel. These Israelites remained faithful to the first six books of the Bible, and followed their religion strictly.

When the Jews returned from their Babylonian exile, they brought with them a religion that had developed and grown, and they despised the Israelites who had stayed at home, many of whom had intermarried with the pagans. The Jews called these people Samaritans.

Some Samaritans still live in Israel. They worship on Mount Gerizim and follow only the books of Moses and Joshua.

Sidon (p.605)

Sidon, or Zidon as it was also known, was originally the name for the country of Phoenicia. Later the name was applied only to a port city of Phoenicia located on the Mediterranean Coast, west of Palestine. Sidon is now called Saida and is a city of Lebanon.

The inhabitants of Sidon and Tyre, another Phoenician port, became rich and famous by exporting their Tyrian dye. This purple coloring was made from the murex, a small sea snail that defends itself by squirting a white liquid from its body. When exposed to light and air, this liquid turns purple and permanently stains any fabric it touches.

The name Sidon is from a Phoenician word for fishery, and indeed the town had been a fishing center and a seaport in Canaanite times. Although Sidon was in the land belonging to the Israelite tribe of Asher, the city was never conquered by the Hebrews. (See Tyre.)

Swine (p. 598)

Swine, or pigs, would not have been kept by Jewish farmers, for Jews were forbidden by the law of Moses to eat pork, the meat of swine. The swine probably belonged to Greeks, many of whom lived in Gadara, a city of Decapolis. Pork was a popular food among the Greeks.

Sycamore (p. 622)

This tree was not what we call a sycamore today, but was the sycamore fig, sometimes called the mulberry fig. Its fruit looks like that of the fig tree, but it is so bitter that it was eaten only by the poor. Its leaves look like those of the mulberry tree.

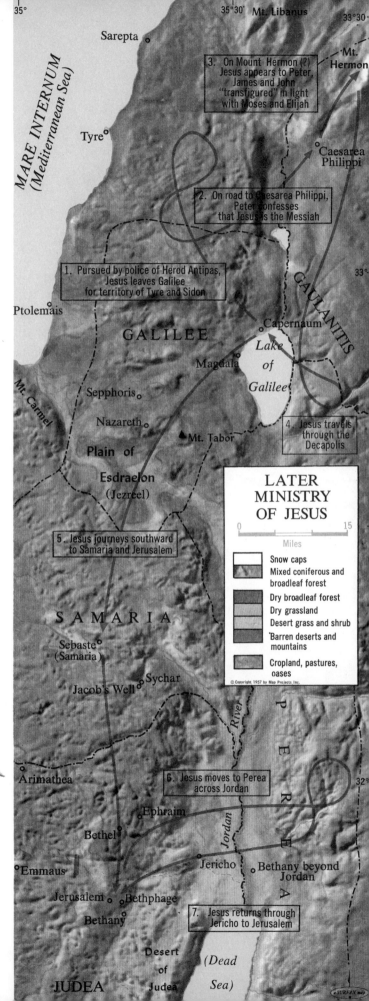

35°   35°30' Mt. Libanus   33°30'

Sarepta

MARE INTERNUM (Mediterranean Sea)

3. On Mount Hermon (?) Jesus appears to Peter, James and John "transfigured" in light with Moses and Elijah

Mt. Hermon

Tyre

Caesarea Philippi

2. On road to Caesarea Philippi, Peter confesses that Jesus is the Messiah

1. Pursued by police of Herod Antipas, Jesus leaves Galilee for territory of Tyre and Sidon

33°

GAULANITIS

Ptolemaïs

GALILEE   Capernaum

Lake of Galilee

Magdala

Mt. Carmel

Sepphoris

Nazareth

Mt. Tabor

4. Jesus travels through the Decapolis

Plain of Esdraelon (Jezreel)

LATER MINISTRY OF JESUS

0   15
Miles

5. Jesus journeys southward to Samaria and Jerusalem

Snow caps
Mixed coniferous and broadleaf forest
Dry broadleaf forest
Dry grassland
Desert grass and shrub
Barren deserts and mountains
Cropland, pastures, oases

© Copyright 1957 by Map Projects Inc.

SAMARIA

Sebaste (Samaria)

Jacob's Well   Sychar

River

P E R E A

Arimathea

6. Jesus moves to Perea across Jordan

32°

Ephraim

Bethel

Jordan

Emmaus

Jericho   Bethany beyond Jordan

Jerusalem   Bethphage

Bethany

7. Jesus returns through Jericho to Jerusalem

Desert of Judea

(Dead Sea)

JUDEA

Tares (p.594)

In biblical times, tares meant any vicious weeds that choked out food crops. The tares mentioned in this parable were probably a rye grass that grew as a weed in grain fields. It had red or purple spikes that resembled the grain stalks among which it grew, making it hard to get rid of. Sometimes a fungus infected the weed, making the kernels poisonous. If the infected rye grass kernels were mixed with food grain, anyone who ate them could become quite ill.

Thomas (p. 624)

Very little is known about the apostle Thomas. His name, *Toma*, meant twin, but the Bible does not mention the name of the other twin.

Thomas is also sometimes called "Doubting Thomas," because he did not believe that Jesus had risen from the dead until he had actually seen him. That name is still used today to refer to a skeptical person.

Torturers (p. 610)

The unmerciful servant who was delivered to the torturers was probably sent to be whipped. The Jews did not practice torture, though in some cases Jewish wrongdoers were scourged, or whipped. The word torturers probably meant the men who did the whipping.

The whipping was done under very careful safeguards that were written into the law of Moses. One such safeguard against cruelty required that the punishment be carried out under the eyes of the judge who delivered the sentence.

Some of the people of Eastern lands, notably the Assyrians, were greatly feared because of the horrible tortures they inflicted on criminals and on their enemies.

Transfigure (p. 606)

To transfigure means to change a person's or thing's appearance. At the Transfiguration of Jesus, his face "shone like the sun," thus changing his appearance.

Tyre (p. 605)

Tyre, located on the Mediterranean Sea, was an important Phoenician seaport. In the time of Jesus, Tyre was already an old city, for it had probably been settled around 2000 B.C.

The town prospered because of successful trade and commerce. At first, its fortunes were based on the dye Tyrian purple. (See Sidon.) When the sea snails from which the dye was made disappeared from their waters, the people of Tyre sent out ships to find more of the small creatures. These ships founded colonies around the Mediterranean, some as far away as Spain. From the colonies the Phoenicians brought home new goods to sell to neighboring countries.

The people of Tyre had been traders even before they built their shipping fleet. They had begun their trading using caravans, some of which had brought goods from as far away as India.